FROM WHERE I STAND

IN THE CITY

MARIMBA BOOKS
An imprint of Kensington Publishing Corp. and Hudson Publishing Group LLC
850 Third Avenue, New York, NY 10022

Text copyright © 2008 by Cheryl Willis Hudson. Illustrations copyright © 2008 by Nancy Devard.

All Kensington titles, imprints, and distributed lines are available at special quantity discounts for bulk purchases for sales promotions, premiums, fund-raising, and educational or institutional use.

Special book excerpts or customized printings can also be created to fit specific needs.
For details, write or phone the office of the Kensington special sales manager:
Kensington Publishing Corp., 850 Third Avenue, New York, NY 10022, attn: Special Sales Department, 1-800-221-2647.

MARIMBA BOOKS and the Marimba Books logo are trademarks of Kensington Publishing Corp. and Hudson Publishing Group LLC.

ISBN-13: 978-1-60349-002-3   ISBN-10: 1-60349-002-
First Marimba Books Printing: November 2008

10 9 8 7 6 5 4 3 2 1

Printed in United States of America

From where I stand

I see mostly feet.

Coming and going,

they never miss a beat.

I see swift ones, slow ones,

average, thin, and stout.

I see lean ones, in-between ones,

and sleepy ones, no doubt.

There are scruffy slides with toes turned in.

There are shiny pumps and moccasins.

I see tired feet,
And sometimes socks with holes.

I see tan, bare legs
And sparkling, painted toes.

Feet shift and they shuffle,

and they bounce out the door.

They tap and they slide,

and they move to and fro'.

I see thigh-high boots,

and lots of sneakers everywhere!

Some pass much too quickly
As they move from here to there.

But sometimes in the bustle
I catch a glimpse and find

**A pair of pint-sized shoes
Just about the size of mine.**

For me it's a neat surprise
Because for a change
I see someone's eyes.
I see the rest of her body, too.
Not just socks, feet and shoes.

To see a whole person
Is an extra special treat.

**From where I stand
This makes my day complete!**